MONSTERS
of Class 7

by Michael Ratnett
illustrated by June Goulding

COOL KIDS
PRESS

for Mary Jenkins, and all exasperated teachers

Copyright ©1995 by M. Ratnett & J. Goulding

ISBN: 1-56790-513-7

New Printing 1998

COOL KIDS PRESS

Division of BookWorld Press, Inc.
1933 Whitfield Park Loop   Sarasota, FL 34243 USA

Printed in Singapore

Ratnett, Michael.

    Monsters of Class 7 / by Michael Ratnett ; illustrated by June Goulding.
        p.   cm.
     Summary: Princess Priscilla, the polite new student in Miss Bramble's class of monstrous children, is not quite what she appears to be.
    ISBN 1-56790-513-7
    [1. Behavior--Fiction.   2. School field trips--Fiction.
3. Extraterrestrial beings--Fiction.] I. Goulding, June, ill.
II. Title.
PZ7.R1938Mo   1995   95-10614
[E]--dc20   CIP
                                               AC

Miss Bramble was a very nice teacher. But her Class 7 children were monsters who never said "please" nor "thank you," and who did just what they wanted, and who always wiped their noses on their sleeves. And Miss Bramble would not have missed any of them if they had been carried off by aliens.

So she was very pleased when a nice new girl turned up in class one day who wasn't a bit monstrous.
"My name is Princess Priscilla," said the new girl.

"Goodness," said Miss Bramble. "A princess! Say hello, everyone."
"Hi," said Class 7.
"How do you do?" Princess Priscilla politely asked.

Miss Bramble wanted to show Princess Priscilla how much she liked her, so she planned a special day out. There was a bus waiting at the school gates.

Miss Bramble and Class 7 piled in, and they all roared down the road, all the way to...

THE BEACH!

It was a beautiful, sunny day. Class 7 had loads of horrible fun.
But Princess Priscilla did not have loads of fun.

"I've done this before, Miss," she said.
"Oh dear," said Miss Bramble. "Then we'll just have to go somewhere else, won't we?"

Miss Bramble found a ship, and they all piled aboard. Class 7 hadn't ever been on a ship before. It was great!

The ship sailed north until they came to...

Class 7 thought that the Arctic was a marvelous place, and they had lots of terrible fun. They fought with snowballs, and built snowmen, and looked for polar bears.
But Princess Priscilla didn't think the Arctic was such a marvelous place.

"I've done this before, Miss," she said.
"Oh dear," said Miss Bramble. "Then we'll just have to go somewhere else, won't we?"

Miss Bramble borrowed an airplane, and soon they were all whizzing south. Class 7 liked the airplane even more than the ship.

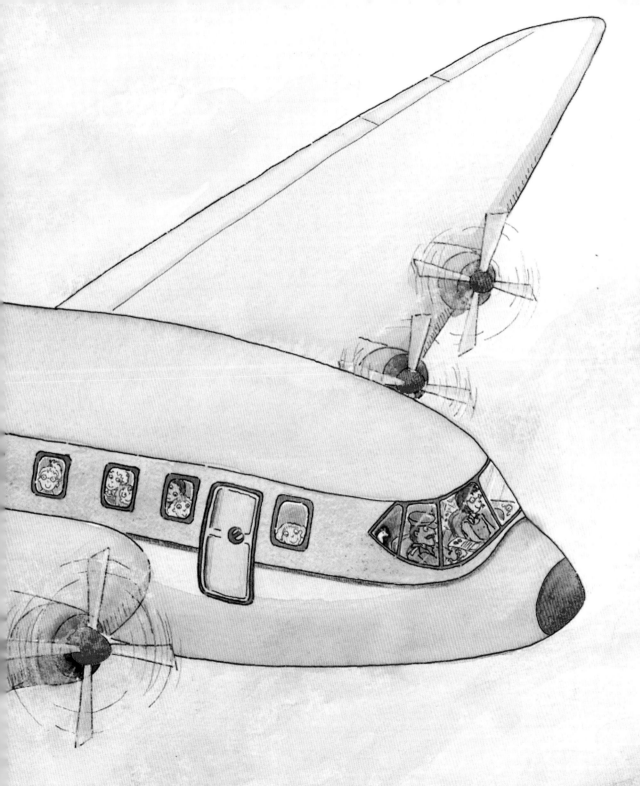

They flew on until they were right over the equator, and then they landed in...

THE JUNGLE!

Class 7 thought the jungle was wonderful. There were all sorts of
animals and birds to play with. They went wild!
But Princess Priscilla didn't go wild.

"I've done this before, Miss," she said.
"Oh dear," said Miss Bramble. "Then we'll just have to go somewhere else, won't we?"

Miss Bramble and Class 7 joined a caravan and traveled across the desert. Camel-riding was very difficult, but after a while they got the hang of it. Soon they reached...

THE PYRAMIDS!

Class 7 thought the pyramids were brilliant! They ran up and down them, and built their own, and they had masses of outrageous fun.

But Princess Priscilla didn't think the pyramids were so brilliant.
"I've done this before, Miss," she said.
"Oh dear," said Miss Bramble. "Then we'll just have to go somewhere else, won't we?"

Miss Bramble knew where there was a rocket ship. In a flash they were all zooming through space.

They soared past the moon, and kept going until they landed on...

MARS!

Mars was the best place ever and Class 7 loved it! They explored the red Martian caves, and clambered over the blue Martian rocks, and looked for purple Martian monsters, and they had heaps of disgusting fun.

But Princess Priscilla just smiled quietly.
"I've done this before, Miss," she said.
"Now, really," said Miss Bramble. "You can't possibly have done this before!"
But then Princess Priscilla stepped out of her disguise!

She was a Martian monster!
"Run!" cried Miss Bramble. But it was too late. In the wink of an eye, they were surrounded by monsters who grabbed the children in their great big purple paws!

"Well done, Priscilla," said the Martian Monster King. "These are the naughtiest ones you've ever brought back."
"It was nothing, Dad," said Princess Priscilla. "After all, I've done this before!"
All the other monsters gave her three hearty cheers.

The Martian Monster King liked sorting out naughty children. It was his hobby. He put all of Class 7 to work in his filthy old castle. They had to do all the cleaning and the cooking and the washing. It took them six weeks just to scrub clean the Martian Monster King's super smelly socks!

And all that time Miss Bramble was allowed to do nothing except gobble chocolates, sleep on feather beds, and watch intergalactic television, because she was such a nice teacher.

When the Martian Monster King thought the children were ready, he let Miss Bramble load them back into the rocket ship and take them home.

And when they got back to Earth, things were very different. The Class 7 children had become perfect angels who always said "please" and "thank you," and did just what they were told, and never ever wiped their noses on their sleeves.

And what about Princess Priscilla? Well, right now she's busy looking for a new school to visit. So if you and your friends are monstrous in class, and one day a new kid turns up who is very well behaved, WATCH OUT!